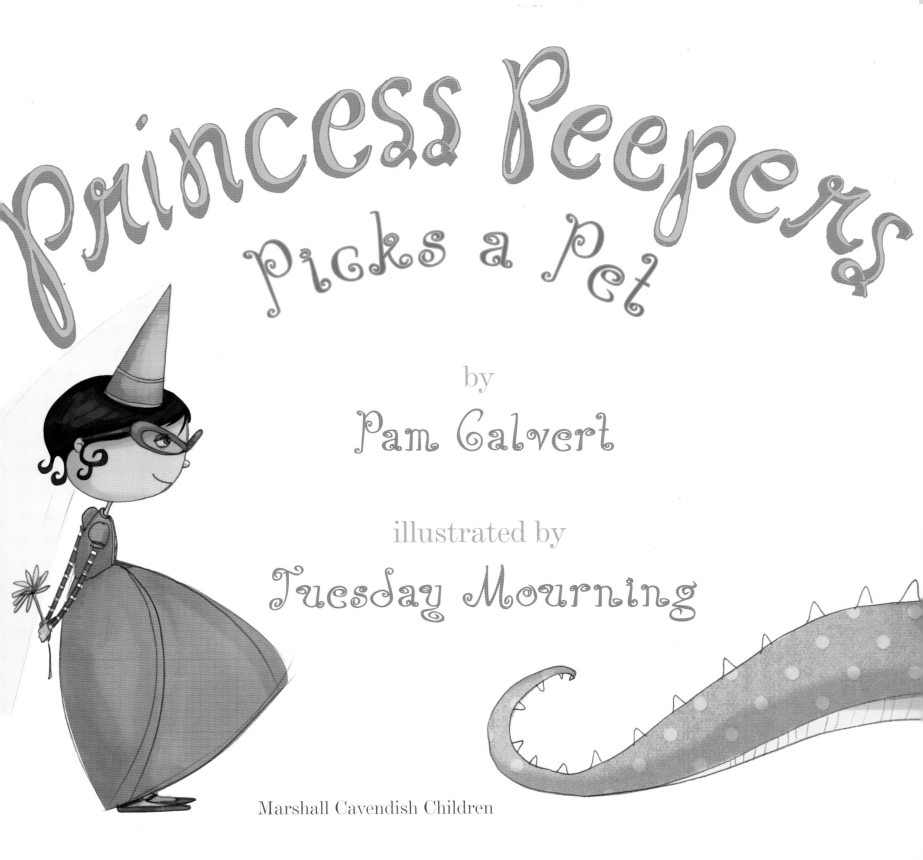

Princess Peepers
Picks a Pet

by

Pam Calvert

illustrated by

Tuesday Mourning

Marshall Cavendish Children

Marshall Cavendish Corporation, 99 White Plains Road, Tarrytown, NY 10591
www.marshallcavendish.us/kids

Library of Congress Cataloging-in-Publication Data
Calvert, Pam, 1966–
Princess Peepers picks a pet / by Pam Calvert ; illustrated by Tuesday Mourning. — 1st ed.
p. cm.
Summary: When Princess Peepers loses her glasses, she mistakes a dragon for a unicorn and
enters it in the pet show at the Royal Academy for Perfect Princesses.
ISBN 978-0-7614-5815-9
[1. Princesses—Fiction. 2. Dragons—Fiction. 3. Pets—Fiction.] I. Mourning, Tuesday, ill. II. Title.
PZ7.C138Ps 2011
[E]—dc22
2010010056

The illustrations are rendered in graphite, digital painting, and collage.
Book design by Anahid Hamparian
Editor: Marilyn Brigham

Printed in China (E)
First edition
10 9 8 7 6 5 4 3 2 1

 **Marshall Cavendish**
Children

In memory of my mother-in-law, Kay Calvert,
who shared the love of writing with me
—P. C.

To my loving parents who have always encouraged,
supported, and believed in me
—T. M.

Princess Peepers never quite fit in at the Royal Academy for Perfect Princesses.

When the princesses played dress up, Peepers wore a safari costume with zebra glasses.

When they hosted a tea party, Peepers arrived on her skateboard, accidentally crashing into the table.

When they practiced their posture in the garden, Peepers hung upside down from a tree to straighten her back.

So, when the Grand Matron announced that they were going to put on a pet show, everyone squealed in excitement. Everyone except for Princess Peepers.

She raised her hand. "Grand Matron? I don't have a pet."

"That's strange," the princesses whispered.

"Well," said the Grand Matron, "you may help me behind the curtain instead."

Fairy dust, Peepers thought. *I want to be in the show, too.*

After class, the princess ran to her room. Maybe a bug from her collection would do.

"Perfect!" she cried.

But when Peepers brought her pet to practice, Grumbelina said, "Bugs are not allowed. Only pets with two or four legs, not six." The other princesses agreed.

Princess Peepers wished she had a pet like that. What could she do?

Since watching dragonflies buzz always helped her think, she decided to walk to the pond.

At the pond, Peepers still couldn't think of any good ideas. But just as she was about to leave, she noticed a perky frog perched on a lily pad. "Holy pumpkins!" Peepers cried. "How many legs do you have?" She counted, "One-two-three-four. YES!" Peepers scooped up the frog and skipped to the theater.

But when she showed the frog to the princesses, they turned up their noses.
"Yuck! A pet is cuddly, not slippery."
"Yes," said another princess. "And it should have feathers or fur—
not slime."

Princess Peepers drooped as she left the theater. Where could she find a cuddly pet? One with two or four legs that had feathers or fur?

Maybe in the forest, she thought. So Peepers headed outdoors once again.

Princess Peepers walked along a trail. She was so deep in thought that she accidentally tripped on a log. Her glasses flew off her nose!

"Jeepers!" Peepers cried. "Now I'll never find a pet."

As Peepers got up, she felt something nuzzle her cheek. She giggled, gazing at a large animal. "Could you be my pet?" She counted its feet. "One-two-three-four! Perfect! You're not slimy, are you?" She rubbed the animal's belly. "Ohhh, you're softer than a horse!" She patted its head and felt a long horn. Stroking the creature's side, she felt wings.

"You must be a flying unicorn!"
The unicorn nudged her.
"My! Your teeth are a little sharp for a unicorn. But I still think you're perfect."

Maybe the unicorn is hungry,
Peepers thought. She picked a large
flower and lifted it to his mouth.
The unicorn snorted. The flower caught
on fire.

"Holy fireball! You're a strange
unicorn!" The princess stamped out
the flames.

Gently, Peepers kissed her pet to calm him. She wrinkled her nose. "Oh, stinky troll's feet! You need a bath. Your fur feels like it's caked with hard, scaly mud!" The princess climbed on his back. "There isn't time to wash you. We need to get to the pet show. Quick!"

Back at the theater, the show was about to begin. But where was Princess Peepers?

"Maybe it's better she's not here," Grumbelina said. "What would she bring next? A troll?" The other princesses laughed.

Princess Black-pearl balanced on a tightrope as her parrot flew around her.

Grumbelina did a perfect pirouette with her posh poodle.

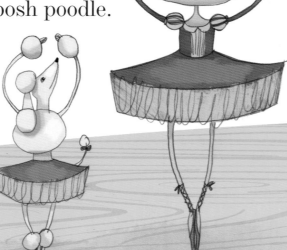
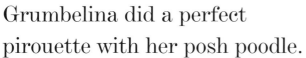

Princess Ponytail performed tricks with her horse.

After the last act was finished, all the pets and owners lined up to take a bow. That's when Princess Peepers flew into the theater.

She soared over the audience.

WHOOSH!

The crowd screamed in delight!

Finally, Peepers and her pet landed. The princess took her place next to the other contestants. *Will the princesses like my pet?* she wondered. *Will I win a prize?*

The Grand Matron began announcing the awards.

"The Most Talented award goes to . . .
Princess Black-pearl and her pet parrot."

"The Prettiest Pet award
goes to . . . Princess Grumbelina
and her pet poodle."

"The Most Athletic
Pet award goes to . . .
Princess Ponytail
and her pet horse."

"And the Most Unusual Pet award goes to . . .

. . . Princess Peepers and her pet DRAGON!"

"Oh, magic mirrors!" Peepers cried. "My pet isn't a unicorn?"

The princesses giggled.

The Grand Matron offered a pair of glasses to Princess Peepers. "It helps to have an extra pair handy, my dear."

Peepers put on the glasses and gazed at her new pet, seeing him clearly for the first time.

"You're more perfect than I could ever have imagined!" she said.

And so, Princess Peepers and her perfect pet lived happily ever after.